Drugs in Sport

Nicolas Brasch

NELSON CENGAGE Learning

Australia • Brazil • Japan • Korea • Mexico • Singapore • Spain • United Kingdom • United States

Drugs in Sport

Fast Forward
Turquoise Level 17

Text: Nicolas Brasch
Editor: Bec Quinn
Design: James Lowe
Series design: James Lowe
Production controller: Seona Galbally
Photo research: Fiona Smith
Audio recordings: Juliet Hill, Picture Start
Spoken by: Matthew King and Abbe Holmes
Reprint: Siew Han Ong

Acknowledgements
The author and publisher would like to acknowledge permission to reproduce material from the following sources:
Photographs by AAP Image/AFP/Niurka Barroso, pp17 top, back cover bottom; AAP Image/AP Photo/Tony Feder, p18; Corbis/Leo Mason, p14; Corbis/Tim de Waele, p16; Getty Images/AFP p7; Getty Images/AFP/Javier Soriano pp 4, 8; Getty Images/AFP/Jeff Haynes, p5; Getty Images/AFP/Ramzi Haidar, pp front cover right, 11, 23 right; Getty Images/AFP/Rob Elliot, pp 14-15; Getty Images/AFP/Romeo Gacad, pp 3, 9; Getty Images/Allsport/Simon Bruty, pp 10-11, 23 centre bottom; Getty Images/Graeme Robertson, p20; Getty Images/Phil Cole, pp front cover left, 19, 23 left; Getty Images/Thomas E Witte, p6; iStockphoto.com, p13; Photolibrary/Alamy/Doug Steley, pp 17 centre; back cover top; Photolibrary/Science Photolibrary/Adam Hart-Davis, pp 12-13; Photolibrary/Science Photolibrary/Dr P Marazzi, p12.

Text © 2007 Cengage Learning Australia Pty Limited
Illustrations © 2007 Cengage Learning Australia Pty Limited

Copyright Notice
This Work is copyright. No part of this Work may be reproduced, stored in a retrieval system, or transmitted in any form or by any means without prior written permission of the Publisher. Except as permitted under the Copyright Act 1968, for example any fair dealing for the purposes of private study, research, criticism or review, subject to certain limitations. These limitations include: Restricting the copying to a maximum of one chapter or 10% of this book, whichever is greater; Providing an appropriate notice and warning with the copies of the Work disseminated; Taking all reasonable steps to limit access to these copies to people authorised to receive these copies; Ensuring you hold the appropriate Licences issued by the Copyright Agency Limited ("CAL"), supply a remuneration notice to CAL and pay any required fees.

ISBN 978 0 17 012653 3
ISBN 978 0 17 012621 2 (set)

Cengage Learning Australia
Level 7, 80 Dorcas Street
South Melbourne, Victoria Australia 3205
Phone: 1300 790 853

Cengage Learning New Zealand
Unit 4B Rosedale Office Park
331 Rosedale Road, Albany, North Shore NZ 0632
Phone: 0508 635 766

For learning solutions, visit cengage.com.au

Printed in China by 1010 Printing International Ltd
6 7 8 15

Evaluated in independent research by staff from the Department of Language, Literacy and Arts Education at the University of Melbourne.

Drugs in Sport

Alan Trussell-Cullen

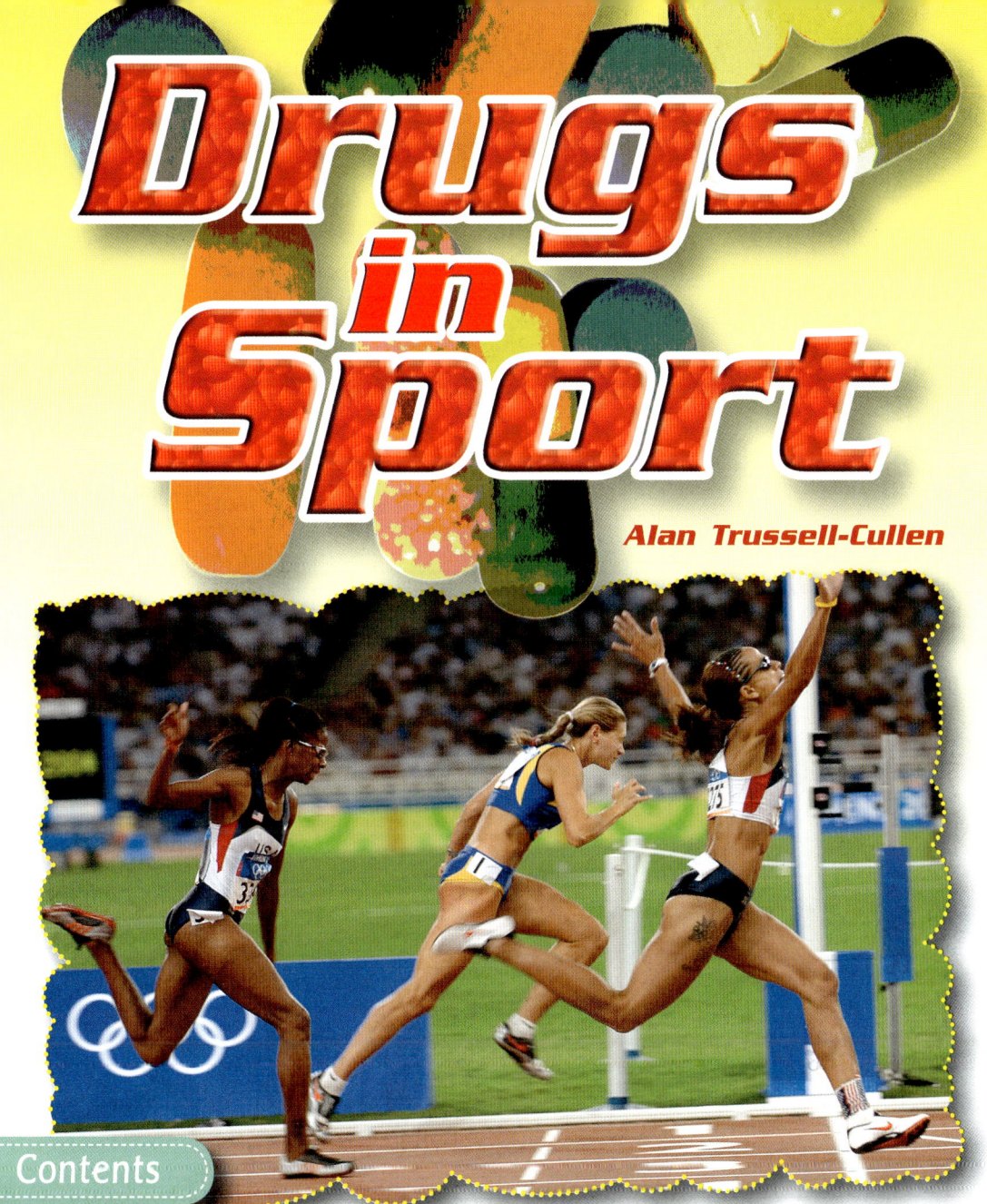

Contents

Chapter 1	**Performance-Enhancing Drugs**	4
Chapter 2	**Why Sportspeople Use Drugs**	6
Chapter 3	**Why Drugs in Sport Are Bad**	10
Chapter 4	**Getting Rid of the Drugs**	14
Chapter 5	**Dwain Chambers**	18
Chapter 6	**Conclusion**	22

Chapter 1

PERFORMANCE-ENHANCING DRUGS

Some sportspeople try to improve their chances of winning by using drugs.

The drugs sportspeople use aren't drugs that drug takers in the community take, and they aren't drugs that change people's thoughts.

They're drugs that **enhance** a person's performance.

Drugs that enhance performance
make a person's body go faster,
or become stronger than it normally would be.
These drugs are known as performance-enhancing drugs.
There are many different performance-enhancing drugs.
These drugs have no place in sport today.

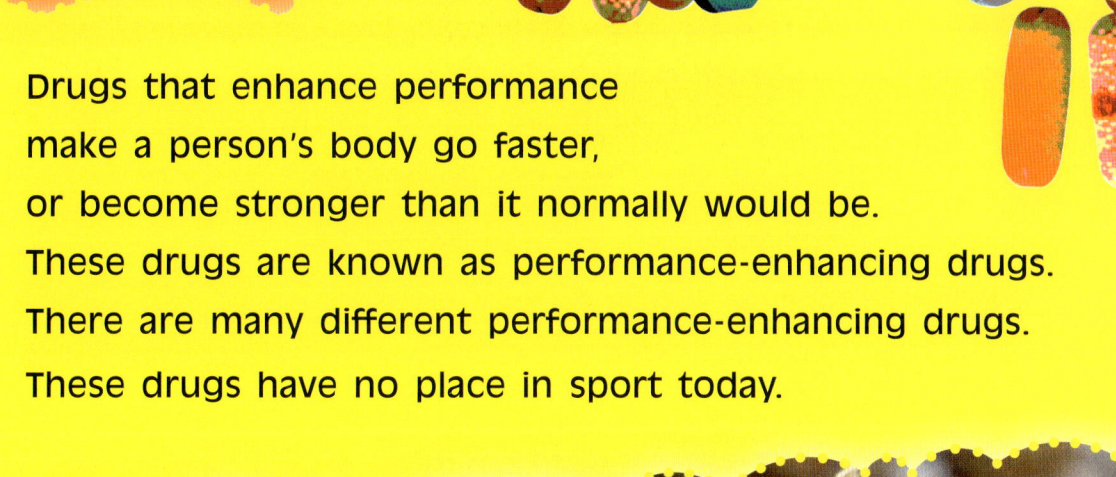

WHY SPORTSPEOPLE USE DRUGS

Sportspeople who use performance-enhancing drugs take them to improve their performance.

They want to improve their performance because of the **glory** and rewards that come from being a sporting success.

Serena Williams' natural talent has made her a sporting success.

People who reach the top of a sport can become famous and earn a lot of money.

David Beckham has reached the top of his sport without using performance-enhancing drugs.

Some sportspeople who use performance-enhancing drugs take them because they don't have the natural talent to reach the top. They need extra help to win.

Some sportspeople take performance-enhancing drugs to compete against other drug takers.
They believe they also have to take the drugs to win.

Chapter 3
WHY DRUGS IN SPORT ARE BAD

There are two main reasons why performance-enhancing drugs should not be taken by sportspeople.

First, they make sporting contests unfair.

2006 Tour de France: 13 cyclists banned

They give the drug takers an unfair **advantage**.

Sportspeople who take drugs can run faster, or lift heavier weights, or compete for longer. That's unfair.

It's not what sport is about.

Seoul Olympics: Ben Johnson banned

Athens Olympics: Ferenc Gyurkovics banned

Second, performance-enhancing drugs **cause** side-effects. Some cause only a bit of pain to the people taking them, but many cause damage to a person's body.

Side-effects include:
- stomach pain
- nausea
- acne

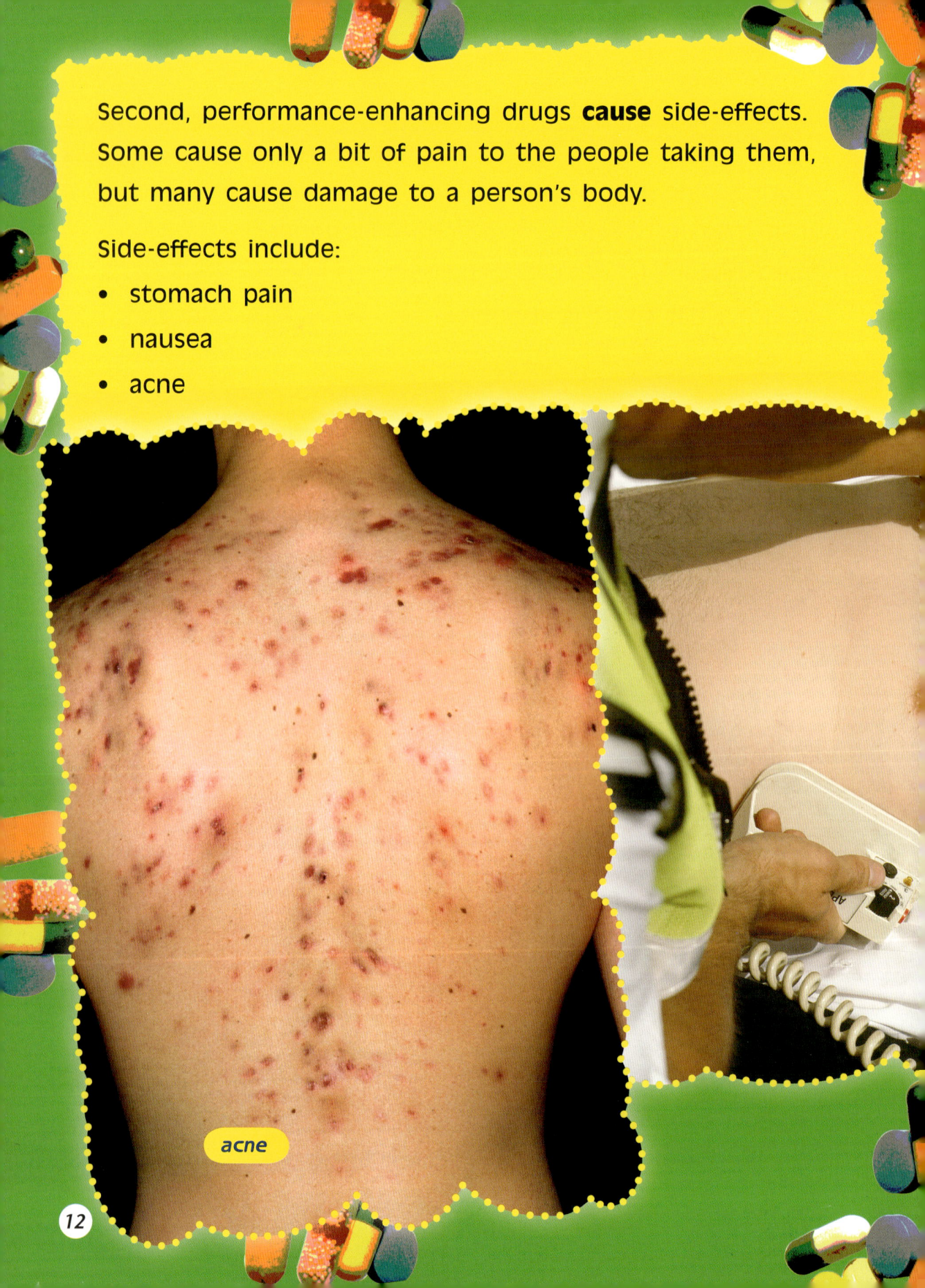

acne

- fertility problems
- deep voice (for females)
- stunted growth (for teenagers)
- stroke
- seizure
- heart attack.

In some cases, sportspeople have died from these side-effects.

Chapter 4

GETTING RID OF THE DRUGS

Sporting groups and governments around the world are trying to get rid of performance-enhancing drugs in sport.

First, they want to make sure that sporting contests are fair.

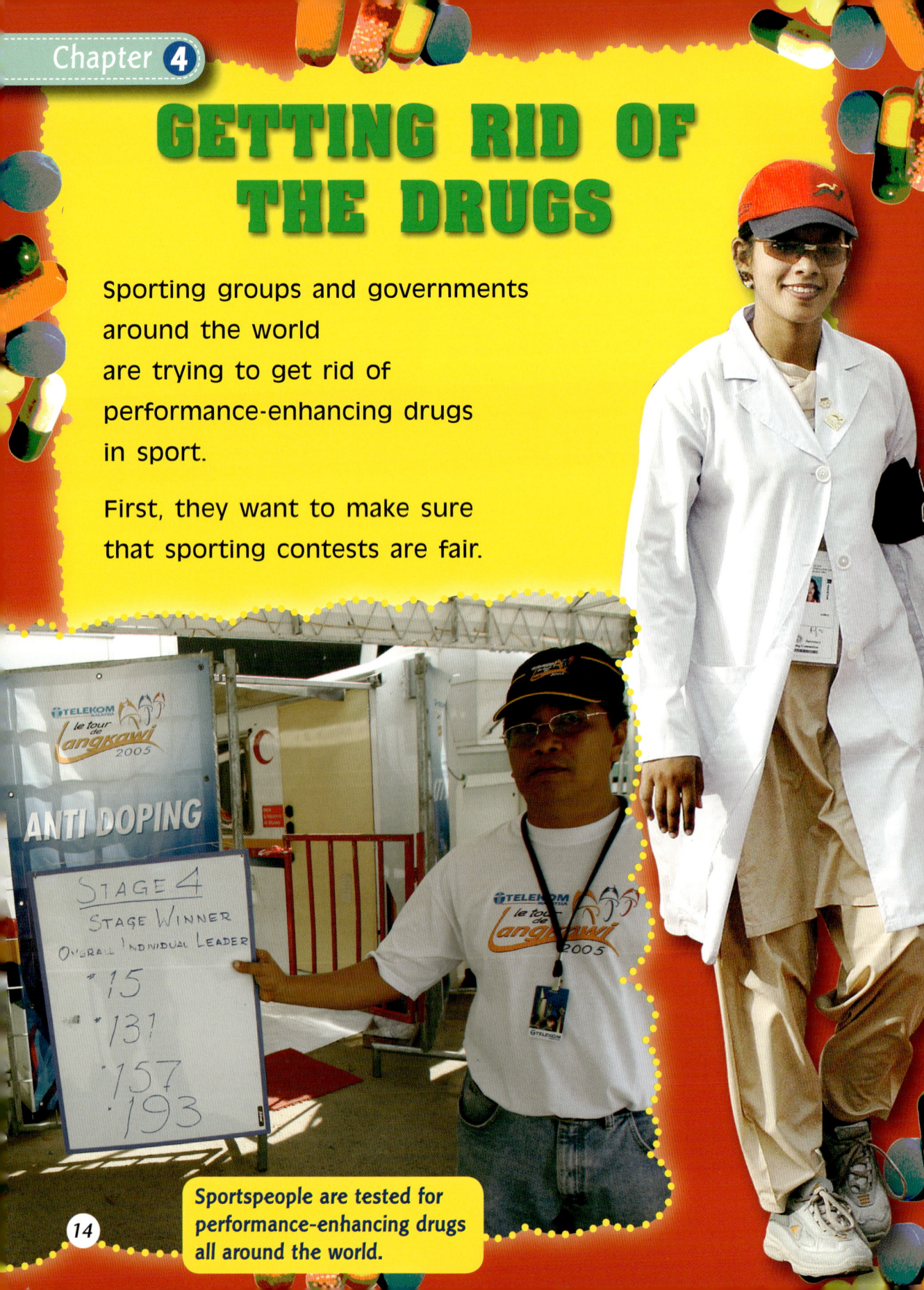

Sportspeople are tested for performance-enhancing drugs all around the world.

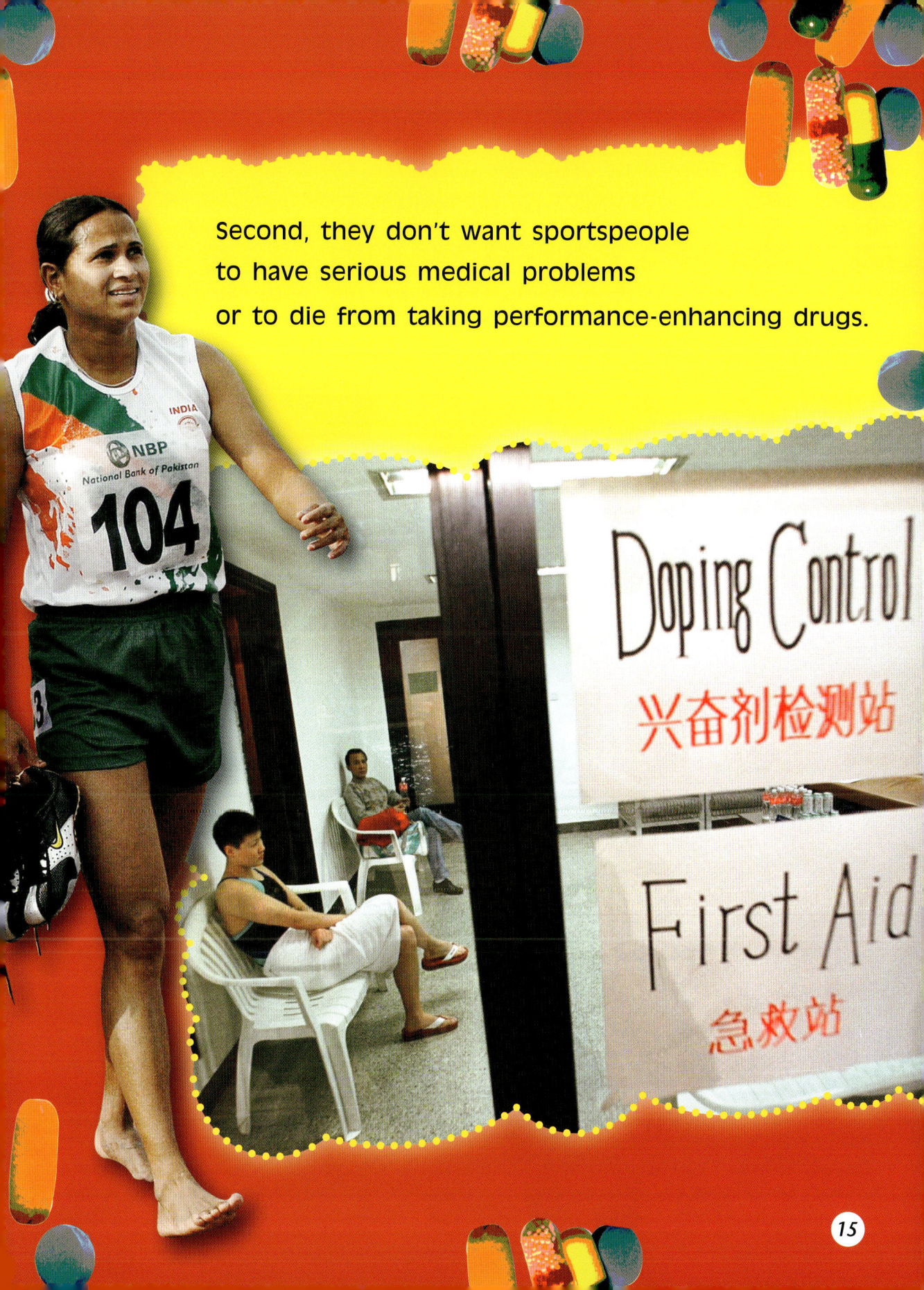

Second, they don't want sportspeople to have serious medical problems or to die from taking performance-enhancing drugs.

To help get rid of drugs in sport, leading sportspeople may be tested to see whether or not they have **traces** of performance-enhancing drugs in their bodies.

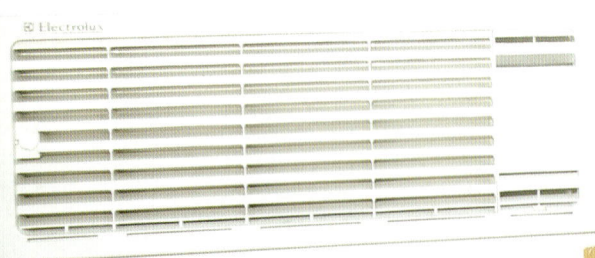

a cyclist waits for a drug test during the Tour de France

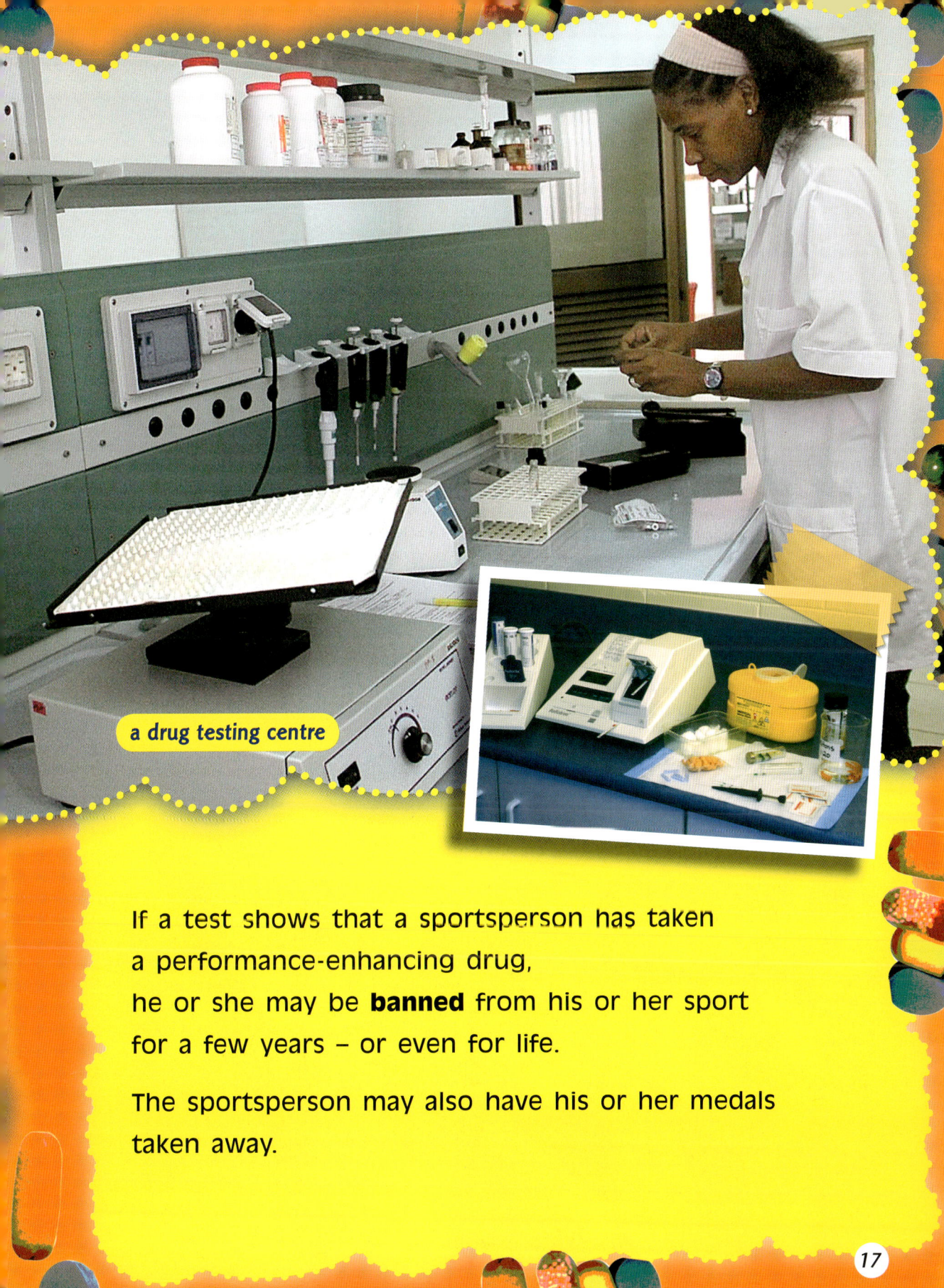

a drug testing centre

If a test shows that a sportsperson has taken a performance-enhancing drug, he or she may be **banned** from his or her sport for a few years – or even for life.

The sportsperson may also have his or her medals taken away.

Chapter 5

DWAIN CHAMBERS

Dwain Chambers is a British sprinter who took performance-enhancing drugs.

At one stage, he held the world record for the 100-metre sprint.

Dwain was banned from his sport for two years because he was caught taking performance-enhancing drugs.

Dwain Chambers won gold in the men's 100-metre final at the Goodwill Games in Brisbane in 2001.

In an interview Dwain Chambers gave in 2005, he said:

"Everything I had worked for since I was 14 years old had totally **vanished**...
It's not the way I want people to see me –
I've got a black mark against my name now
as a drugs cheat..."

Dwain Chambers waiting for the result of his trial

"There's nobody else I can blame,
for the simple reason that I made those decisions
to go forward as I did...
I was young, I didn't think about life
and the ups and downs that could occur."

Chapter 6

CONCLUSION

Performance-enhancing drugs are banned in sport because they give the sportspeople who take them an unfair advantage over other sportspeople.

They can also cause a lot of harm to people who take them.

They can even cause people to die.

Sporting groups and governments work hard to catch sportspeople who take performance-enhancing drugs.

People who are caught may be banned from **competing** in their sport.

23

Glossary

advantage   a lead; benefit

banned   stopped from competing

cause   bring about

competing   taking part in a contest

enhance   improve

glory   praise

traces   small amounts

vanished   disappeared; gone away

Index

Athens Olympics   11

Beckham, David   7

Chambers, Dwain   18–21

Seoul Olympics   11

side-effects   12–13

Tour de France   10, 16

Williams, Serena   6